W9-CMS-783

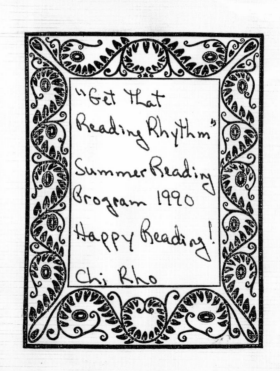

"Get That
Reading Rhythm"
Summer Reading
Program 1990

Happy Reading!

Chi Rho

A Little Night Music

CHARLES MICUCCI

MORROW JUNIOR BOOKS / NEW YORK

Printed in Hong Kong.

1 2 3 4 5 6 7 8 9 10

Library of Congress Cataloging-in-Publication Data
Micucci, Charles.
A little night music / Charles Micucci.
p.   cm.
Summary: At night while everyone is asleep, a cat plays the violin
and dances.
ISBN 0-688-07900-8. ISBN 0-688-07901-6 (lib. bdg.)
[1. Cats.—Fiction.] I. Title.
PZ7.M5834Li 1989
[E]—dc19   88-505   CIP   AC

For my little friend
who says "meow"

Would you like to know a secret?

Promise not to tell the dog that chases me,

or the children who pet me, or the lady who reads us stories.

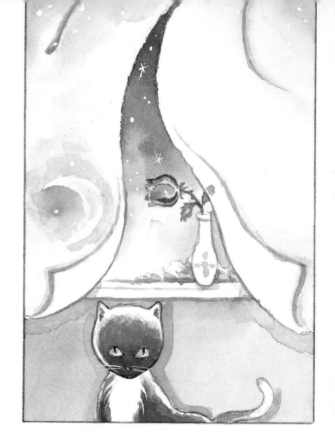

Late at night, when everyone is asleep, I wake up.

I look right and left to make sure no one is around.

Then I sneak over to the sofa,
dig my paws deep behind the cushions—
past a forgotten toy airplane,
past a hidden dog biscuit,
past a lost earring—
and pull out . . . my violin!

I raise it to my chin and play.
My tail starts to twitter.
My paws start to tap.
I start to dance.

I spin on the sofa

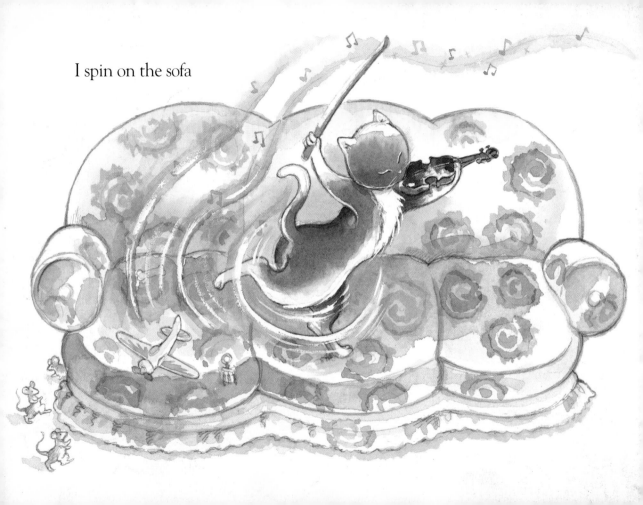

and whisk across the windowsill.

I bop over the
bookshelf…

prance under
the piano…

twirl on the
television . . .

and shuffle past
the sleeping dog.

I dance all over the house.
And everywhere I dance,
I play a little night music.

The music fills the air.

It muffles every other sound—
the clock ticking,
the people snoring,
the footsteps coming down the hall.

Footsteps coming down the hall?

It's the dog!
What is he going to do?

"Shall we dance?"

"I'd love to."

At first, we just dance in a circle.

But soon we are dancing
all over the house.

Our shadows spin on the wall.
And everywhere we dance,
we sing a little night music—